T0198560

THE STORY OF THE PIG

Alero Macaulay

AuthorHouse™
1663 Liberty Drive
Bloomington, IN 47403
www.authorhouse.com
Phone: 1 (800) 839-8640

This book is printed on acid-free paper.

ISBN: 978-1-7283-5151-3 (sc)
ISBN: 978-1-7283-5150-6 (e)

Library of Congress Control Number: 2020905308

Print information available on the last page.

Published by AuthorHouse 03/19/2020

authorHOUSE®

Once upon a time, a long time ago, animals lived like human beings live now.

They walked upright, talked, worked, and lived in houses like human beings.

One day, the rain stopped raining, and the land of animals dried up and a famine devastated the land of animals, and caused great grief to the animals. It changed the way they lived forever.

This is the story of what happened to the Pig and the Tortoise.

During that time, in the land of animals, Pigs were the merchants. They sold goods and were also the first animals to practice loaning other animals money. Pigs were seen as the wealthy animals because they had a lot of stores, land and money.

Well when the famine devastated the animal land, other animals went to the Pigs for assistance.

One of those animals was the Tortoise.

There was this Tortoise named Wisdom. Wisdom owned a restaurant but because of the famine he was unable to get fresh fruits and vegetables for his restaurant because the crops had dried up and died. He was also losing customers because the other animals were unable to afford to come to his restaurant because of the famine.

So Wisdom, the Tortoise went to his good friend Gift, the pig. Wisdom asked Gift for fresh fruits and vegetables. And Gift said "sure Wisdom, I still have some fruits and vegetable but the price is higher now, because I am not producing crops and have to buy my fruits and vegetables from another land".

Wisdom said "well Gift, I do not have any money to give you, because I haven't received any customers since the famine devastated our land and this food that I need is actually for my family to eat and not for the restaurant".

Gift said "oh goodness, I did not know you were in such a great need for food. What I can do is give you enough fruits and vegetables, both for your family and your restaurant, on credit, but you have to pay me back next month. Hopefully by then you will be able to make some food to sell and pay me for the fruits and vegetables. Is that a deal?"

Wisdom the Tortoise said "yes. Thank you so much." And they shook each other's hand.

Well one month passed, and unfortunately Wisdom, was unable to sell his food, and instead the family just used the fruits and vegetables to feed themselves because the animal land was still stricken by famine.

Well a week after one month passed. The pig, Gift, came to Wisdom's house. He knocked on the door and asked for Wisdom. Wisdom came to the door and said "I am so sorry Gift, I do not have the money to pay you back, please give me more time. Perhaps by the end of this month I will have your money."

The Pig, Gift, said "oh ok Wisdom, I understand, but please try to make plans to get the money to me because I also have to buy fruits and vegetables from another land so I can sell to other animals and so my family can live."

Wisdom, said "thank you Gift, I understand, and I will try."

Well another month passed and still Wisdom was unable to get the money. This time, he sent his daughter to tell Gift what was happening and to explain that they have not been able to sell any food in the restaurant and he is planning on trying to go to another land to sell food so he can get money to pay back Gift.

Gift was upset, but he said "ok, tell your father I understand, I will give him another month, and then I will come to the house to get the money."

Wisdom's daughter said "thank you." Then she went to tell her father Wisdom.

Wisdom was relieved but still worried. In the next month, he went everywhere to try to sell his food but no one would buy it because they were afraid to spend their money because of the famine.

One month passed again, and the pig, Gift came to Wisdom, the Tortoise's house as he stated he would.

Wisdom heard him coming, and told his daughter to tell him that he was not home but had travelled. He turned his belly up and pretended to be grounding stone, and asked his daughter to grind pepper and tomatoes on him. When the pig, Gift came, the daughter did as her father had instructed. She said "my father is not here and I am just grinding some tomatoes and pepper." The pig, Gift, was furious he picked up what he thought was the grounding stone and threw it over the fence into the landfill- where trash was thrown and demanded to speak to Wisdom. Oh no, Wisdom's daughter panicked and began to cry. We do not have your money and the little money that we do have was hidden in that grounding stone. The pig, Gift, did not know that what Wisdom's daughter was saying was a lie. He did not know that the thing he had thrown into the landfill was neither a grounding stone nor anything that could store money but rather Wisdom, the tortoise.

The pig, Gift, ran to the land fill to look for the grounding stone, and other Pigs came to help and they have been looking ever since, that is why the Pig looks through trash and dirt until today.

So next time you see a pig looking through trash, you know the story of how it became that way.

You may wonder what happened to Wisdom, the Tortoise, I am not quite sure. Some say that his shell cracked but he was able to escape the sight of the pig, Gift, who was searching for him in the landfill. And that is why tortoises have cracked rough backs. Others say, although the tortoise made it alive and escaped the sight of the pig, he was never able to recover and that is why Tortoises do not walk upright and walk so slowly. Maybe one day we will find out what really happened to the Tortoise.

Good night.

Color Me Page

About the Author

I have been writing since I was a child. Believing that all things in this universe are connected, I aspire to continue to study all subjects, although my love is language, philosophy, religion, sociology, history, science and law. I think the mind should always remain curious, which inspires knowledge. My formal education is in international politics and law. However, I have worked as an English teacher. As an Albert Schweitzer Fellow in law school, I created a creative writing and critical thinking program for children-teaching in Junior Secondary/Middle School and later in the YWCA Community center-teaching children from 5 years to 10 years old. This book is dedicated to my mother, maternal grandmother and maternal great grandmother. Stories were created from their imagination and passed down from generation to generation. Their stories created my lenses.

Printed in the United States
By Bookmasters